The Princess
& the
Pepperoni Pizza

A "What Happens Next?"™ Fairy Tale

Amy Joy &
Hans Christian Andersen

Book design, cover art, illustrations, and Pepperoni Pizza storyline by Amy Joy, © 2011 Amy Joy. "The Princess and the Pea" (1835) by Hans Christian Andersen.

Second Edition, Copyright © 2017 Amy Joy

ISBN-10: 1542601061
ISBN-13: 978-1542601061

tenterhookbooks.com

For all the little princesses & princes of the world.
Because having choices is a very good thing.

How to read this book

This is not an ordinary story! It is broken into many sections. At the end of each one, you will be asked to make a choice about what you would like to see happen next.

Choose wisely! It will affect the outcome of your story—which may not end up having anything to do with a princess and a pizza, depending on what you choose.

Good luck!

The Prince Meets the Water-logged Princess

ONCE upon a time there was a prince who wanted to marry a princess; but she would have to be a real princess. He travelled all over the world to find one, but nowhere could he get what he wanted. There were princesses enough, but it was difficult to find out whether they were real ones. There was always something about them that was not as it should be. So he came home again and was sad, for he would have liked very much to have a real princess.

One evening a terrible storm came on; there was thunder and lightning, and the rain poured down in torrents. Suddenly a knocking was heard at the city gate, and the old king went to open it.

It was a princess standing out there in front of the gate. But, good gracious! What a sight the rain and the wind had made her look. The water ran down from her hair and clothes; it ran down into the toes of her shoes and out again at the heels. And yet she said that she was a real princess.

"Well, we'll soon find that out," thought the old queen.

What happens next?

ȡ) *To have the queen put a pea in the princess's bed, turn to page 3.*

ȡ) *To have the queen put pizza in the princess's bed, turn to page 28.*

The Queen Puts a Pea in the Princess's Bed

But the old queen said nothing, went into the bedroom, took all the bedding off the bedstead, and laid a pea on the bottom; then she took twenty mattresses and laid them on the pea, and then twenty eider-down beds on top of the mattresses.

What happens next?
- *To have the princess climb up and go to sleep, turn to page 30.*
- *To have the princess not be able to climb to the top of the pile of mattresses, turn to page 4.*

3

The Princess Can't Climb Into Bed

"This is ridiculous!" the princess said as she tried desperately to climb to the top of the stack of mattresses. "They should at least have given me a ladder! WOOOOAH!" With that, the princess tumbled back down to the floor.

What happens next?

    ↄ *To have the princess pull off the top mattress and lay it on the floor to sleep for the night,* *turn to page 5.*

    ↄ *To have the princess get fed up and storm out of the castle,* *turn to page 32.*

The Princess Tries to Sleep on the Floor

Carefully, the princess attempted to pull the top mattress off the stack to lay it on the floor to sleep for the night. But as she did, something warm and gooey suddenly fell down on her head.

"What is this?" she cried. Gingerly, she touched the top of her head. Something wet and slimy met her fingers. She pulled her fingers away and looked at them. They were covered in bright red yuckiness. That's when she caught a whiff. "Pizza?"

She ran to the mirror to look. Sure enough, there were pepperonis in her hair, and cheese was now sliding down her back. She pulled off several ooey, gooey pieces, but she couldn't stop the sauce from running down her face.

What happens next?

- *To have her run to the bathroom to clean up, turn to page 7.*
- *To have her storm out of the castle, turn to page 32.*

The Princess Runs to the Bathroom to Clean Up

The princess ran from the bedroom, but as she did, she suddenly realized that she had no idea where the bathroom was. So instead, she ran back to where she had last seen the prince and queen.

Thankfully, they were still there. Well, thankfully, she thought until the queen started laughing!

"My dear," the queen said, "you certainly do look a sight!" She turned to her son. "Well, surely you can see now that this young lady is not a princess."

"What I see, mother, is a beautiful young lady with pizza on her head! You wouldn't know anything about this, would you?"

"Richard! How could you even think of such a thing?"

Richard frowned. He knew his mother had been known to involve herself in stranger things than this. "My lady," he said to the princess. May I show you to a place where you can get cleaned up?"

The princess felt a little unsure. Maybe I should just leave now? she thought. But she was tired, and unlike his strange mother, the prince seemed genuinely concerned about her well-being.

What happens next?

∾ To have the princess leave now, turn to page 20.

∾ To have the princess follow Richard, turn to page 9.

The Princess Follows Prince Richard

"I am so very sorry," the prince said as he led her down a long hallway. "Please, let me make it up to you."

The princess didn't respond. She wasn't sure yet what to make of the prince. He led her to a bathroom and showed her where she could find towels to wash up.

Afterward, he found his servant, George, and asked for his assistance. "Please take the young lady— " The prince looked at the princess suddenly. "Oh dear," he said. "I'm so very sorry, but I don't even know your name.

"Olivia," she answered.

The prince bowed. "Prince Richard, honored to make your acquaintance, my lady."

Olivia blushed.

Prince Richard turned to his servant. "As I was saying, George, please take Princess Olivia to the castle boutique to find some new clothes that suit her."

Princess Olivia smiled. Thank goodness, he noticed, she thought. Not only were her clothes now stained with pizza, but they were still wet from the rainstorm she'd come through earlier that evening.

George bowed to the prince, and he and the princess headed to the boutique.

Inside, George called to the boutique manager, Franz, to help the princess select a new wardrobe.

"And what does the lady require?" Franz asked.

What happens next?

℞ To have her choose a fancy gown, turn to page 38.

℞ To have her choose bedclothes, turn to page 11.

The Princess Chooses Bedclothes

"Well, Franz," Olivia said, "I still haven't slept. So some comfortable bedclothes would be lovely.

"Ah yes," Franz replied. "We have quite a wonderful selection! Were you thinking of something more formal or fun?"

What happens next?
  ✂ *To choose fun pajamas, turn to page 14.*
  ✂ *To choose formal pajamas, turn to page 12.*

The Princess Chooses Formal Pajamas

"Formal pajamas would be lovely, Franz."

"As you wish, my lady," Franz said, and he left and returned a moment later with several long, elegant nightgowns.

"Oh my!" the princess exclaimed. "They are all so beautiful! How will I choose?"

"Might I suggest this one, madam?" Frantz said, holding up a long, silky purple gown with satin lace.

"Oh Franz, it's wonderful," she replied.

"Would you like to try it on?" he asked.

"Most certainly," she answered.

Franz showed her to a dressing room and hung the

gown on a hook inside. "One moment, before you change," Franz said. He left and returned again with a matching long, purple robe. "For modesty's sake, you will want this to cover yourself as you walk about the castle."

"Oh, thank you so much, Franz."

She pulled on the gown and robe, and they fit splendidly. It was such a perfect ending to an otherwise imperfect day. When she exited in the dressing room in her new gown and robe, the royal servant, George, was there to greet her.

"The prince asked me to see you to your new sleeping quarters, ma'am."

"Thank you, George."

George led her then to a very different room than where the pizza incident had taken place, and he assured her that there would be no more shenanigans that evening.

Indeed, he was right. That evening, she slept surprisingly well. And in the morning, she joined them all for pancakes before they provided her assistance in finding her way home.

And while the princess never forgot the crazy pizza incident, she didn't hold a grudge about it either.

THE END

The Princess Chooses Fun Pajamas

"Fun pajamas sound great, Franz. I could use some fun after the crazy night I've had!"

"A wonderful choice, madam," Franz said, and he whisked away to find her some fun pajamas.

Franz returned a moment later with his arms full of possibilities: fuzzy pajamas covered in little lambs, lightweight pjs covered with images of flip flops, and a pair of footy pajamas.

"Oh yeah," the princess said. "I'm all about those footy pajamas!"

"You have exceptional taste," Franz replied without a hint of sarcasm.

"Thank you."

He showed her to the dressing room, where she returned a moment later in pink and purple footy pajamas. As she left the dressing room, she saw that the prince had returned as well.

What happens next?

⇛ *To have the prince think she looks adorable, turn to page 16.*

⇛ *To have the prince think she looks ridiculous, turn to page 18.*

The Prince Thinks the Princess Looks Adorable

"Oh my goodness!" the prince exclaimed. "That has got to be the cutest thing I have ever seen!"

Princess Olivia blushed.

"Would you like me to show you to your room now? We have others—so you won't have to go back to the pizza disaster room," he said, smiling.

Olivia was having such a good time now, she had almost forgotten all about the pepperoni pizza ordeal. "Hmm…I'm not sure," she said. "I'm kind of awake now." Her stomach growled loudly. "And I guess I'm hungry too."

"Ah, yes, well we can fix that. Anything in particular

you'd like to eat?"

"Promise you won't laugh?" the princess asked.

The prince nodded.

"Pizza sounds delicious." She smiled, embarrassed.

The prince laughed suddenly and then quickly covered his mouth. After all, he had promised that he wouldn't laugh, but it was funny.

She smiled back, and he took her hand and led her to the royal kitchen, where they found more pizza. This they took to the royal TV room, where they sat up all night, eating pizza and laughing at their favorite shows. They quickly found that they had a lot in common, so they became great friends who visited each other daily.

And they are still great friends to this day.

THE END

The Prince Thinks the Princess Looks Ridiculous

The princess thought that her day was beginning to improve, but as she saw the prince's face, she knew she had gotten her hopes up too soon.

At first, he looked stunned.

Then all at once, he started to laugh.

And laugh.

And laugh.

And laugh.

And then he was rolling on the ground, laughing hysterically.

The princess turned and looked at Franz, who looked just as surprised as she was.

The prince continued to laugh and roll, until the princess had enough. She turned back to Franz. "Thank you, Franz; you have been very kind to me," she said. "Would you please now show me to the door?"

George, who was standing nearby—also witnessing the ridiculous affair—now stepped forward. "It would be my pleasure to escort you, madam."

"Thank you," she replied, and the two of them stepped right over the prince, who was still making a fool of himself by rolling on the floor.

George saw to it that the princess arrived home safely that evening, where she was greeted warmly by her loving parents.

As for the prince, he was left alone to think about what he and his mother had done. And, we can hope, they learned from their mistakes. For if they didn't, we can imagine it's quite possible that they lived unhappily ever after.

THE END

The Princess Leaves the Castle

"Thank you," the princess said. "But I think I've had enough for tonight. I've had a short break from the weather, and I think I better be heading home now."

The prince was sad to see the princess depart so quickly, but he understood. She wasn't the first young lady his mother had driven from the castle with her crazy antics.

The prince summoned his guards to see the princess safely home, but before he bid her goodnight, he asked, "Would you mind if I called on you sometime?"

The princess thought about it for a moment. Despite

all she'd been through that evening, the prince had been kind to her and seemed genuinely concerned about her welfare. "Yes," she answered. "That would be lovely."

What happens next?

ℂ *To have the prince visit, turn to page 22.*

ℂ *To have the princess notice something strange about her hair when she gets home, turn to page 23.*

The Prince Visits the Princess at Her Castle

A few days later, the prince visited the princess at his castle. Away from his nutty mother, the queen, the couple got along splendidly.

The prince began riding out to the castle to visit the princess every few days, and within months, the happy couple was engaged to be married. A year after the crazy pizza incident, the prince and princess married and lived happily ever after.

But each time they eat pizza, they still can't help but laugh.

THE END

The Princess Notices Something Strange About Her Hair

The princess had no sooner arrived home when she noticed something very unusual about her hair. "The pizza," she said. "It must have done something to it…"

She yelled *hello* to her father and mother as she ran to the bathroom to see what was going on with her hair.

What happens next?
&cx; *To have her hair look awful, turn to page 24.*
&cx; *To have her hair look beautiful, turn to page 26.*

Something Goes Wrong with the Princess's Hair

The princess looked into the mirror and gasped. "Oh my goodness!" she cried. "MOM! MOM!"

The queen came running. "What on earth? Oh my goodness!" the queen exclaimed. She watched with horror as the princess touched her head and her beautiful locks began to fall to the ground.

The princess began to weep. "Oh mother," she said, flinging herself into her mother's arms. "It's been horrible, horrible! And now this! What will I do? My hair!"

The queen was heartbroken seeing her daughter in such distress. She had obviously been through quite

24

an ordeal this evening. She summoned her hairdresser immediately, who set the young princess up with a long, elegant wig. "Back in my day, the queen explained, "it was a great luxury to wear a wig. Only the finest royalty wore them."

This was little consolation to the princess at first, but she had been begging her mother to let her do something dramatic with her hair for some time now. The queen had always refused before, but given the circumstances, she permitted her daughter this luxury.

The princess soon became known for her wonderful, luxurious, and often quite colorful wigs, and she became a great inspiration to those who had lost their hair due to various sicknesses. Meanwhile, the queen organized food research that revealed various unhealthy toxins in some of our favorite foods. She used this research to improve food safety so that everyone in her kingdom would live, long and healthy lives.

As for poor prince Richard and his mother, well, let's just say their story doesn't have quite so happy an ending.

THE END

The Princess's Hair Looks Beautiful

The princess ran to the mirror and stood there, shocked. Her hair had never looked so soft and shiny. She ran her fingers through it. It was like silk.

She didn't know what to think. Could the queen have had any idea? What was in that pizza?

She ran to show her mother.

"That's amazing!" her mother said. She couldn't stop running her fingers through her daughter's hair. "Simply incredible!"

Over the next week, her mother sent away for countless pizzas from all over the country and put her kingdom's best scientists to work researching the ingredients and their affects on human hair. What they found resulted in an entire line of specialty hair products that boost the kingdom's previously desperate economy.

Meanwhile, the prince came to visit, and he and the princess hit it off immediately. He began riding out to visit her every day, and before long, they were happily married. And, given the great success the princess and her mother had with their new line of hair-care products, the princess made up with Prince Richard's mother, and they all lived happily ever after.

THE END

The Queen Puts Pizza in the Bed

"I'll have the servants go make up a room for you," the old queen said, and she left the room. But she didn't go straight to the bedroom. On the way, she stopped at the kitchen— where, on the counter, sat a box half-full of pepperoni pizza.

"Are we going to do the ol' pea in the bed trick again, your majesty?" an old servant named George asked.

The old queen smiled and eyed the pizza. "I have a better idea." She snatched up the box, waved for the servants to follow, and headed up to the guest room.

In the room, she made her way to the bed, lifted the fancy, white, ruffled covers, and pulled up the top mattress. "Yes, this will do nicely," the queen said.

"George, open that box and pull out the pizza."

"Yes, your highness."

"Now bring it over here and shove it in."

"Into the bed, mum?" George asked.

"You heard me!"

"Yes, mum."

Into the bed it went an icky, gooey, sticky mess. The red sauce would surely stain the pretty, white sheets.

Yet the queen smiled as she let the top mattress drop back down with a splat. Then she gave the servants a look that made cold chills run down their arms. "Now we'll see if she's a real princess!" she said.

George—who had worked with the queen almost since the time she took the throne—was used to her strange ways. He simply looked to the other servants, shrugged, and shook his head lightly so the queen couldn't see.

What happens next?

∾ To have the princess smell the pizza as soon as she walks into the bedroom, turn to page 64.

∾ To have the princess get into bed without noticing the pizza, turn to page 66.

∾ To have her take one look at the stack of mattresses and decide to sleep on the floor, turn to page 5.

The Princess Sleeps on the Pea

On this the princess had to lie all night. In the morning she was asked how she had slept.

"Oh, very badly!" said she. "I have scarcely closed my eyes all night. Heaven only knows what was in the bed, but I was lying on something hard, so that I am black and blue all over my body. It's horrible!"

What happens next?

∿ *To have this be proof that she is a real princess, turn to page 31.*

∿ *To have the princess storm out of the castle, turn to page 32.*

Proof that she's a Real Princess

Now they knew that she was a real princess because she had felt the pea right through the twenty mattresses and the twenty eider-down beds.

Nobody but a real princess could be as sensitive as that.

What happens next?

    ᡆ *To have them live happily ever after, turn to page 33.*

    ᡆ *To have the princess think the prince and his family are bonkers, turn to page 34.*

The Princess Storms Out

"I have never been treated so badly in my entire life!" the princess said. "Good riddance!" And with that, she picked up her things and stormed out of the castle.

When the princess returned home, word spread quickly about the crazy treatment she received at the old castle, and not another princess ever visited there again.

THE END

Happily Ever After

So the prince took her for his wife, for now he knew that he had a real princess; and the pea was put in the museum, where it may still be seen, if no one has stolen it.

There, that is a true story.

THE END

The Princess Thinks the Prince's Family is Bonkers

"You put a pea in my bed!" the princess exclaimed. "Are you insane? Did you ever consider that maybe I didn't sleep well last night because I was in a strange place with strange people who pile eighteen mattresses on top of each other and expect me to climb to the top? And did you think that maybe it's because I was cold and uncomfortable because you didn't offer me any fresh clothes so I had to sleep in the wet ones I came in last night?"

"Eighteen mattresses," the queen mumbled to herself. How ridiculous. I'd never use less than twenty."

The princess was beside herself. She was cold. She

was wet. She was tired. She was sore. And she had had just about enough.

What happens next?
∾ To have the princess storm out of the castle, turn to page 32.

∾ To have the prince apologize, turn to page 36.

The Prince Apologizes

The princess headed for the door, but the prince intervened.

"Princess! Wait!"

The princess huffed loudly. "Why?"

"Please can we talk?"

The princess frowned.

"I am so very sorry," the prince said. "Please, let me make it up to you."

But the princess said nothing.

"Some dry clothes perhaps?" the prince suggested.

"Well, it'd be a start," the princess answered, looking down at her clothes that were still cold and wet.

"Fine then." He gestured to his servant, George. "Take this young lady—" The prince looked at the princess suddenly. "Oh dear," he said. "I'm so very sorry, but I don't even know your name.

Again the princess looked annoyed. "Olivia," she said.

"I'm Richard," the prince said, bowing to the princess. "It's nice to formally make your acquaintance."

The prince turned to his servant. "As I was saying, George, please take Princess Olivia to the castle boutique to find some dry clothes that suit her."

George bowed to the prince, and he and Princess Olivia headed to the boutique. Inside, George called to the boutique manager, Franz, to help the princess select a new outfit.

"And what does the lady require?" Franz asked.

Princess Olivia looked to George and shrugged. "I have no idea what Prince Richard has planned for the day."

"Prince Richard is a kindly gentleman," George said. "I am sure he will follow your desires."

What happens next?

ʕ *To have her choose a fancy gown, turn to page 38.*
ʕ *To have her choose shorts and a t-shirt, turn to page 56.*

Princess Olivia Chooses a Gown

"A gown would be lovely, Franz. Thank you."

"As you wish, my lady," Franz said as he bowed. "Would you mind if I take your measurements?"

"That would be fine," Princess Olivia agreed.

Franz pulled a tape measure from a pocket and quickly made note of various measurements. "I'll return shortly," he said then, exiting.

The princess smiled politely to George as they waited.

A few moments later, Franz returned with a several garments draped over one arm. He hung them on a nearby rack and selected the first. "What do you think of this one?" he asked, holding out a long, shimmery green dress.

What happens next?

To ask to try it on, turn to page 40.

To ask to see the next dress, turn to page 46.

The Princess Tries on the Green Dress

"Oh yes; it's beautiful," the princess said.

"It will make your eyes sparkle," Franz replied.

The princess blushed. "May I try it on?"

"Of course, my lady. There is a changing room in the back.

Just then, the queen entered. "How is everything going?" she asked.

The princess looked at the queen suspiciously.

"Quite well," her servant, George, answered. "The lady has found a dress to try on.

"Splendid," the queen answered artificially. "Let me take that for you and make sure there's a room prepared for you to change in."

What happens next?

☗ *To allow the queen to take the dress, turn to page 42.*

☗ *To tell the queen no, turn to page 45.*

The Queen Takes the Dress

The princess felt unsure, but she allowed the old queen to take the dress.

The queen winked at Franz as she exited. "I'll be right back," she said.

In the dressing room, the queen pulled a container marked "itching powder" from her bag. She laughed to herself. "Now we'll see if she's a real princess! Only a true princess could have the grace to endure this itch without scratching!" She emptied the contents into the dress and shook off the excess. "Perfect," she said to herself as she hung it on the wall.

She exited the room and returned to where the

princess, Franz, and George awaited. "It's all ready for you, princess."

"Down the hall to the right," Franz directed.

What happens next?

↩ *To have the princess try on the dress, turn to page 44.*

↩ *To have the princess notice the powder, turn to page 53.*

The Princess Tries on the Dress

Princess Olivia found the dressing room easily. The dress hung on the wall opposite the door. She entered, closed the door behind her, and pulled the gown from where it hung.

"Beautiful," she said. She couldn't wait to put it on. She quickly undressed, then pulled the gown from its hanger and stepped into it.

What happens next?

❧ *To have the gown look perfect, turn to page 48.*
❧ *To have her choose another gown, turn to page 46.*

The Princess Tells the Queen No

"Thank you, your highness, but Franz has been doing a great job of helping me, and I think we're all set."

The queen glared at the princess, making her thankful she had declined her offer for assistance.

Franz quickly dashed the princess off to a dressing room where she could try on the new gown.

What happens next?
◽ *To have the gown look perfect, turn to page 48.*
◽ *To have her choose another gown, turn to page 46.*

The Princess Chooses Another Gown

*H*mm... she thought to herself. *This is nice, but not quite what I was looking for.*

"Franz," she called.

"Yes, madam," he answered.

"Do you perhaps have another gown I could try?"

"Yes of course, madam."

In a moment she saw a long, pink dress poking itself above the door of the dressing room as Franz attempted to pass it to her.

"Thank you!" she called back.

This one was a simpler style—but no less elegant—and was exactly what she'd been looking for. This is a dress fit for a princess, she told herself.

She left it on and headed back out of the dressing room to see what Franz thought. Just then, she saw that the prince had returned.

"Wow…" was all he could say.

Princess Olivia blushed.

"Well, I guess that decides it then, we'll have to go dancing."

Olivia grinned. She absolutely loved to dance.

That evening, the prince held a giant ball, and crowds packed into the hall including Olivia's parents—who had been sent word that she was there and doing quite well (they didn't mention the queen's crazy antics). And the prince and princess danced and danced until their feet hurt and their smiles ached.

They became great friends from that day forward, and they lived happily ever after.

THE END

The Perfect Dress

It was perfect. Perfect that is, except that it was a bit itchy. "No matter," she thought. The gown looked beautiful, after all, and plenty of fabrics seem a bit itchy at first.

She ran her fingers through her hair and looked at herself again in the mirror. Franz was right: the color made her eyes stand out brilliantly.

She left the dress on and headed back out of the dressing room to see what Franz thought. Just then, she saw that the prince had returned.

"Wow…" was all he could say.

Princess Olivia blushed.

"Well, I guess that decides it then, we'll have to go dancing," the prince said.

Olivia grinned. She absolutely loved to dance.

What happens next?

- *To have them live happily ever after, turn to page 50.*
- *To have the princess get the itchies, turn to page 51.*

They Live Happily Ever After

That day, the prince and princess danced until their feet ached so badly they couldn't dance anymore. Then the prince saw the princess safely home to her castle, where her mother and father were very happy to see her again.

But the prince called on her each day after, and before long they became very good friends. And they grew up, got married, and lived happily ever after.

And to this day—despite all the pleadings of Richard's mother—when princesses come to call on *their* son, they never, ever put anything under her mattress.

THE END

The Princess Gets the Itchies

The prince and princess headed off to the dance hall, but it wasn't long before the princess started to get a serious case of the itchies.

First it started with a little itch.

Then the itch grew bigger.

And bigger.

And bigger.

And soon she couldn't stand it anymore. She started running around, scratching like crazy. She ran all the way back to the royal boutique, where she found Franz and begged for her old clothes back.

"Unfortunately, my lady, I have sent them off to the

royal laundry."

"Ahhh!" the princess screamed. The itch was enough to drive her insane! She ran out of the royal palace and in fact, all the way back to her kingdom, into her palace and to her royal bathroom, where she pulled off the dress and put herself into the tub for a nice long, warm soak.

The itchies eventually subsided and the princess called the prince to apologize.

What happens next?

 ෆ *To have the itching powder prove she's not a princess, turn to page 72.*

 ෆ *To have Richard try to apologize again, turn to page 74.*

The Princess Notices the Itching Powder

As the princess walked to the dressing room, she noticed something strange: a trail of powder on the carpet. The trail led right into the dressing room and right up to where the dress hung on the wall.

She pulled the dress down and carefully pulled out the hanger. Then she unzipped the back and peered inside.

"I can't believe it!" The powder covered the inside of the dress. "First the stuff with my bed and now this?"

What happens next?

    ᴄ͡ʒ *To have the princess storm out, turn to page 32.*
    ᴄ͡ʒ *To request a different dress, turn to 54 or 76.*

The Princess Requests a Different Dress

She tried to keep calm. Perhaps it was nothing?

"Franz,"

"Yes, madam," he answered.

"Do you perhaps have another gown I could try?"

"Yes of course, madam."

In a moment she saw a long pink dress poking itself above the door of the dressing room as Franz attempted to pass it to her.

"Thank you!" she called back.

This one was a simpler style—but no less elegant—and it was exactly what she'd been looking for. "This is a dress fit for a princess!" she told herself.

She left it on and headed back out of the dressing room to see what Franz thought. Just then, she saw that the prince had returned.

"Wow…" was all he could say.

Princess Olivia blushed.

"Well, I guess that decides it then, we'll have to go dancing."

Olivia grinned. She absolutely loved to dance.

That evening, the prince held a giant ball, and crowds packed into the hall including Olivia's parents —who had been sent word that she was there and doing quite well. (They didn't mention the queen's crazy antics.) And the prince and princess danced and danced until their feet hurt and their smiles ached.

They became great friends from that day forward, and they lived happily ever after.

THE END

The Princess Chooses Shorts and a T-shirt

Princess Olivia thought for a moment. "After all I've been through already, I think I'd really like just to be comfortable," she said.

Franz raised his eyebrows, unsure of what she was getting at.

"I'm thinking shorts and a t-shirt," she explained.

"Ah yes," he said, turning, "I think I have just the thing." He darted into the back of the shop then and returned a moment later with a brightly colored t-shirt and a pair of cut-off jean shorts.

"Perfect," the princess replied. "You don't happen to have a pair of flip-flops to match?"

"I most certainly do. Why don't I show you to a dressing room and then I'll fetch them for you?"

"That would be wonderful, Franz. Thanks so much." The princess was genuinely appreciative. She couldn't wait to get out of her soaked and soiled clothes and into the fresh and fun set Franz had found her.

She quickly changed and then met Franz back in the shop entryway, where he was waiting with a pair of bright red flip-flop sandals. "These are perfect!" she said as she slipped them on.

"Now what?" she asked, turning back to the servant, George, who was still waiting for her.

"Well, my dear, I'm sure that's up to you. Why don't I lead you back to Prince Richard and can decide together?"

"That would be lovely, George. Thank you." She turned back to Franz. "Thanks again for all your help."

"It has been my pleasure," he answered.

She followed George to the royal sitting room, where Prince Richard sat waiting.

"Ah, Princess," he said. "You look lovely."

Olivia blushed.

"But I do believe I may now be overdressed." He gestured to his own royal formal wear.

Olivia made a face. "Sorry about that, but I really needed to put on something comfortable. And besides, it's hard to do much in formal clothes."

"I agree completely," Richard replied. "I'll be happy to change. Any ideas what you'd like to do today? You don't still want to go home, do you? I—I mean, I'll be happy to see you safely there if you think your parents will be worried, but I hope you'll stay a while. I'd love to show you the royal amusement park. Of course, there's also the royal zoo, if you prefer."

"Amusement park? Zoo?" Olivia grinned. Her kingdom was large and bountiful, but she did not have an amusement park or a zoo. "Perhaps I could simply call home and let them know that I am alright and will be home for dinner?"

"Of course," the prince said, smiling happily.

What happens next?

౪ *To visit the royal zoo, turn to page 59.*

౪ *To visit the royal amusement park, turn to page 61.*

The Prince and Princess Visit the Royal Zoo

Prince Richard excused himself to change into shorts, a t-shirt, and flip-flop sandals of his own, and returned moments later to lead Princess Olivia to the royal zoo.

They spent the entire day there. And what a wonderful day it was! The Prince's zoo was open to his entire kingdom, and it was extensive! Ostrich and eagles, panda bears and cheetahs! He showed her them all, told her the stories of how they had acquired each animal, and explained the extensive measures they took to provide each one with a suitable habitat. But her favorite stories where those he told about her about endangered animals he and his parents were working hard to help save.

Olivia loved each animal he showed her. They spent the most time watching the elephants and giraffes because elephants were her favorite and giraffes were his.

Then Richard bought them both royal chocolate chip cookie dough ice cream, which they ate in the beautiful zoo gardens before they made their way back to the castle so that Olivia could head home.

THE END

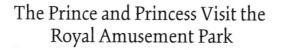

The Prince and Princess Visit the Royal Amusement Park

"The amusement park it is," the prince said, smiling. "I hope you like roller coasters."

The princess grinned. "You betcha!"

The prince quickly excused himself to change and returned moments later in his own jean shorts, brightly colored t-shirt, and flip-flop sandals. Then he took her by the arm and led her out the east wing of the palace.

As they exited, she saw that a small garden opened to an enormous amusement park. People screamed as they flew by on a roller coaster overhead. "It's open to the public, of course," Richard said. "I hope you don't mind. It seemed selfish to keep it all to myself."

"I don't mind at all," she said. In fact she would have thought terribly of him if he were hoarding something so wonderful.

"What first?" Richard asked.

"Do you have a log ride? Olivia asked.

"Of course," he said, smiling. "That's one of my favorites!" He glanced at her clothes. "Of course, that means you'll get wet again."

"This time I don't mind," she smiled back. "Besides, it's a beautiful, sunny day, so I'm sure I'll dry in no time."

"Good point." With that, he took her hand gently and led her to the log ride.

They had a wonderful time. In fact, they enjoyed it so much that they rode it four more times before moving on to another ride.

They rode just about every ride in the park that day. And when they left, she was exhausted.

The prince saw her safely home to dinner that evening, but he called the very next week to invite her back again. And they rode the log ride eight more times that day and ten the week after that.

It became a regular thing for them—visiting the park together and riding the log ride over and over. The two became fast friends. They visited the park together every week that summer. And at least once a week every summer after that.

And to this day, they still visit the amusement park together at least once a week every summer. And the log ride is still their all-time favorite ride.

THE END

The Princess Smells the Pizza

As the princess entered the guest room, a familiar smell found her nose. "Pizza?" she said aloud—though no one was there. "What's up with that? It smells like a pizza party."

She left the room and wandered back down the hall, where she ran into the royal servant, George.

"May I help you, my lady?" he asked.

"Yeah," the princess said, "something's up with my room. It smells like a pizza party."

"I see," George answered. "Perhaps we should inquire about this to the queen?"

George led the princess to the royal sitting room,

where the queen and prince were seated, talking quietly. George cleared his throat, and both turned, surprised.

"Yes?" the queen asked.

"The princess has found her quarters unsatisfactory," George said.

The queen raised her eyebrows.

"With due respect," George said, "she says it smells like a pizza party."

The prince turned and looked at his mother sharply. "Mother!" he said, accusing.

The queen gasped. "I didn't…" she sputtered. But it was obvious from her reaction that she had.

The princess stared on, unsure of what could possibly be going on between them.

At last, the prince turned to the princess. "I'm sorry. My mother has a strange habit of trying to test young girls to see if they are really princesses."

"Well I never!" the queen said, and she left the room.

"She put pizza in your bed," the prince explained.

"She what?" the princess asked.

"She put pizza in your bed," he said again.

What happens next?

꒰ᗢ꒱ *To have the princess storm out, turn to page 32.*

꒰ᗢ꒱ *To have the prince try to make it up to her, turn to page 9.*

The Princess Gets Into Bed Without
Noticing the Pizza

The princess didn't notice anything that night, but she didn't sleep very well either. She kept dreaming about pizza, but she didn't know why.

The next morning, she joined the prince and queen at breakfast.

"How did you sleep, dear?" the queen asked.

"Just fine, thank you," the princess answered.

The queen stirred her tea. "No strange dreams then?"

The princess blushed. "Well, I did dream that I held an enormous pizza party for my kingdom."

The prince choked on his bagel. "Mother!" he

reprimanded. "You didn't!"

"It's the only way to know, son. And now we know. She's a real princess!" the queen answered.

What happens next?

ↀ *To have the prince get excited, turn to page 68.*
ↀ *To have the prince get upset, turn to page 70.*

The Prince Gets Excited

The prince suddenly looked ecstatic. "Really?"

The queen nodded.

"Excuse me," the princess said. "What's going on?"

"There are many old customs in our kingdom," the prince explained, "to test whether a lady is a princess. One is to put a pepperoni pizza under her bed. If she dreams of a kingdom-wide pizza party, she is indeed a princess."

"What? That's ridiculous," the princess said. "I've never heard of anything so absurd since I heard that old pea tale."

"What do you mean absurd?" the queen said. "That

one works every time!"

"Whatever," the princess replied. "I think I've had quite enough." And with that, she gathered her things and headed off.

She quickly found her way back to her kingdom, and she never saw the kooky old queen or her son again.

THE END

The Prince Gets Upset

"Well of course I'm a real princess," she answered.

The prince intervened. "Mother, your ridiculous games don't prove anything. What you need is to be more trusting."

The queen huffed loudly and left the room.

The prince turned to the princess. "I'm sorry. My mother has a strange habit of trying to test young girls to see if they are really princesses."

"Such as?" the princess asked.

The prince looked at her apologetically. "She put pizza in your bed."

"She what?" the princess asked.

"She put pizza in your bed," the prince repeated.

What happens next?

∾ *To have the princess storm out, turn to page 32.*

∾ *To have the prince try to make it up to her, turn to page 36.*

The Itching Powder Proves It

The princess started to explain about the crazy itch that sent her home, but Richard interrupted suddenly.

"Oh my goodness! I can't believe it!" he exclaimed.

"What?" Olivia asked.

"Mother was right," he said.

"What?" she asked again.

"Of course. Why didn't I see it before?" he said.

It seemed to Olivia that Richard was rambling now. "What? What didn't you see?" she asked. He was starting to make her uncomfortable.

"You're not a real princess," he answered.

"What makes you think that?" Olivia asked,

offended.

"Itching powder. It's one of her tests," Richard said. "You scratched!"

"So what?" Olivia said.

"If you were a real princess, you wouldn't have scratched," he said.

"That's ridiculous!"

"You're ridiculous!"

Olivia sighed. "No, Richard. You're ridiculous. Even princesses get the itchies from time to time, and when they do, they have to scratch!"

Richard and Olivia never could come to an agreement on the subject. He was convinced his mother was right, and Olivia became more and more convinced that the two of them were nuts. So eventually, they ended their conversation. And Olivia went on to live a long and happy life, while Richard and his mother the queen, well, they went on to live strangely ever after ever.

THE END

Richard Tries to Apologize Again

"Oh my goodness! I'm so, so sorry!" the prince exclaimed.

"Why? What?" Olivia sputtered.

"It's my mother…Itching powder."

"You're kidding me." At first, Princess Olivia was angry. Then she started to laugh.

And laugh.

And laugh.

And laugh.

And then the prince did too. "Thank you for not getting upset," he said.

"I'm not. I mean, it's not nice. She's a little nutty,

you know."

"Oh, I know!" the prince replied. "So are we still friends?"

"Yes. But you aren't going to take it the wrong way if I insist that you come over to my castle from now on, will you?"

The prince laughed again. "I think that's perfectly understandable."

From that point on, the prince and the princess became very good friends. And as for the queen… well, let's just say her royal subjects do their best to keep on her good side.

THE END

The Princess Chooses a Powder-Free Gown

The princess suspected the queen was up to something, but she decided against making trouble.

"Franz," she called.

"Yes, madam," he answered.

"Do you perhaps have another gown I could try?"

"Yes of course, madam."

In a moment she saw a long, pink dress poking itself above the door of the dressing room as Franz attempted to pass it to her.

"Thank you!" she called back.

This one was a simpler style—but no less elegant—and was exactly what she'd been looking for. This is a dress fit for a princess, she told herself.

She put it on and headed back out of the dressing room to see what Franz thought. Just then, she saw that the prince had returned.

"Wow..." was all he could say.

Princess Olivia blushed.

"Well, I guess that decides it then, we'll have to go dancing."

Olivia grinned. She absolutely loved to dance.

That evening, the prince held a giant ball, and crowds packed into the hall including Olivia's parents— who had been sent word that she was there and doing quite well (they didn't mention the queen's crazy antics). And the prince and princess danced and danced until their feet hurt and their smiles ached.

They became great friends from that day forward, and they lived happily ever after.

THE END

About the Authors

Hans Christian Andersen is a well-known Danish writer whose children's stories, including "The Princess and the Pea" (1835), have been loved for generations. His original story can be found in the following crown-marked sections of the book:

- The Prince Meets the Water-logged Princess
- The Queen Puts a Pea in the Princess's Bed
- The Princess Sleeps on the Pea
- Proof that she's a Real Princess
- Happily Ever After

Amy Joy is a multi-genre bestselling author and illustrator of young adult and children's lit, specializing in unputdownable fiction. Always a fan of stories built through reader choices, Amy Joy brings her own brand of silliness to the genre with "What Happens Next?"™ Fairy Tales. Learn more at tenterhookbooks.com.

Made in the USA
Middletown, DE
10 April 2018